The Texas Hold'em Deaths

Ned Fain, Private Investigator,
Book 4

A Hard-boiled Mystery

Sam Abbott

Sam Abbott

The Texas Hold'em Deaths: Ned Fain, Private
Investigator, Book 4
Copyright © 2015 Liz Dodwell
www.lizdodwell.com

Print ISBN-10: 1939860261
Print ISBN-13: 978-1-939860-26-2

Published by Mix Books, LLC

Table of Contents

One

Being a private eye is not the glamorous, exciting gig that all those Mickey Spillane books made it out to be, and I mean not by a long shot! You spend a ridiculous amount of time doing little or nothing, sitting in a car or a restaurant booth and watching someone else go on with his or her life, while you wish you'd decided to become a proctologist, instead. At least the terrified patients would be entertaining, right?

If you're reading this story, you probably already know who I am, but just in case you're a newbie who picked it up in the doctor's office out of sheer desperation to take your mind off the bad news you're expecting, let me introduce myself. I'm Ned Fain.

I used to be a lawyer for the US Army, a prosecutor, to be precise. I was assigned to the JAG office at mission HQ in Afghanistan to prosecute war crimes, in particular those of our so-called "allies" in the Afghan government and military. I was pretty good at it; my conviction rate was around ninety three percent, not bad in any prosecutor's office, but that is probably the reason why one of my cases decided to blow me up. A grenade was tossed into the latrine with me, while I was on a break from a case before I made my final summation.

The grenade blew off part of my right foot, took about half of my hearing and left me with burn scars over most of my body, including my once-handsome face. My hair, somehow, managed to grow back in, but I'll never manage a beard that doesn't look like prairie grass in a desert.

Anyway, when I got out of the hospital, they gave me an honorable discharge, a small medical pension for my foot and hearing, and sent me home. I tried to go back into law, but I developed a courtroom phobia that made it impossible, so I was doing odd jobs for a year.

Then I was in the wrong place at the wrong time, and saw an old colleague of mine who'd just been murdered. I didn't see the actual killing, but when the cops figured out that I was right and the guy was dead before he fell into the polar bear habitat at the zoo in front of a couple dozen school kids—don't ask—their only real suspect was a pretty schoolteacher, and she tried to hire me as her lawyer. When I explained that I couldn't do it, she made me one more offer: be her investigator and prove that it was the victim's widow who had him killed.

I tried to say no, but like I said, she was pretty, and when she wrote me a check for ten grand as a retainer, I found myself nodding, instead.

Long story short, I did find proof of who killed the guy, and it turned out it was my client. That case left me feeling like a man again, for the first time since that blast. I was still a licensed attorney, so getting my PI license was a snap, and a couple weeks later I was in business. My first "official" case left me with a decent payday and a new secretary/assistant named Sylvi who happens to make The Girl With The Dragon Tattoo look like an amateur with a computer. On top of that, she puts up with me staring at her now and then; oh, yeah, she's a fox!

So back to the present; I was coming off a boring case. Local hotel had noticed that several thousand dollars worth of Top Shelf booze was disappearing every month, and called in yours truly to find out how. I stuck up some sneaky cameras Sylvi found for me, sat and watched endless hours of nothing on an online security video monitoring system, and finally got enough proof that it was the head janitor. He had a nice little racket going, supplying high-dollar liquor to a couple of clubs at bargain prices, but now he was looking at grand larceny charges that would get him a couple years in state. Case closed, and I had just picked up my check. The hotel management was grateful and promised me more work whenever they needed my kind of services. A big hotel does, now and then, so I was in a pretty good mood as I walked out their front door that morning.

Good moods are like weather, and subject to sudden changes. Mine took a nose dive about four seconds after I stepped out into the sunshine, because a scream cracked the air above me, and I looked up just as a man's body hit the concrete right in front of me.

A human body falling from the tenth floor of a hotel goes *splat* when it hits concrete, and all of a sudden I was literally covered in blood and gore. Another freakin' suit ruined, and a dozen people around me started screaming their heads off, while a few of them barfed all over their shoes.

Yeah, mood pretty much ruined.

I wiped my face off best I could with an already ruined sleeve and a hanky, then waited patiently for the cops to get there. A few of the people stayed with me, but most of them took off like rabbits, so when my old pal Mick Mulcahy drove up with a couple cars full of uniforms, I let the others go first.

Five witnesses means five different stories. Two of them insisted that they had looked up just before the scream and saw someone push the guy, and the others all gave different descriptions of what they saw and heard. I replayed the whole scene in my mind, and I was pretty certain that none of them had even noticed the scream; they only looked when the body went *whack!* and a ton of blood splattered all over me. Sadly, though, some people like to grab their fifteen minutes of fame any way they can, so telling their "stories" made them feel important, even if they had to make them up on the spot. Mick and his crew talked to them while the CSI gang took pictures and made measurements. A couple of the uniforms kept the TV crews back, but I could see their cameras aimed our way, trying to get a shot of the body. I kept my back to them; I really hate TV cameras, and being a PI means I need to keep my face out of pictures whenever I can. With one as recognizable as mine, that means I have to work extra hard at staying away from those guys.

When they got done with the bystanders, Mick turned to me.

"Tell me about it, Ned," he said. "Give me the prosecutor's version."

Mick and I had enough history for him to know I'd give an accurate description of events. I pointed at the now covered corpse.

"I'd just come out the door behind me when I heard someone scream, above. I looked up, but didn't see a thing because the body passed my field of vision too fast. I heard it hit, and got splattered with all this muck, and by the time I realized what had happened, he was already looking like that. Well, the blood puddle wasn't that big, yet, but you know what I mean."

Mick nodded. "Think it was suicide?"

I shook my head in the negative. "Suicides don't scream in fear, they yell in anguish or rage. This guy was screaming in terror, but I think maybe he just got too close to the window ledge after too many drinks last night. He wasn't screaming anything like, 'No, don't,' he was just screaming, like an 'Oh, crap!' kind of thing."

Mick sighed. "Okay. Usual spiel, we'll be in touch if we need anything else, yada, yada yada. Take it easy, Ned, and say high to Sylvi for me."

"Will do," I answered, and went to my car. I dug an old blanket out of the trunk, one I kept there for emergencies, and put it over my seat before I got in, then drove back to my office. I lived in the back room, there, so I could shower and change as soon as I arrived.

It's days like that one that make me wish I still kept some beer in the fridge, but I knew if I ever went down that road again, it might never end. I didn't want to go back there, so I kept bottles of root beer in there, instead.

Sam Abbott

Two

Sylvi was at her desk when I parked in front of the building, and looked up as I entered. Her eyes went from surprise to shock in a split second, and she was up and by my side a second after that.

"Omigod, omigod, Ned, are you hurt? What happened?"

"It's not my blood, Syl, chill out. Some guy fell out a window at the hotel as I was leaving and missed me by about three inches. He splattered me with himself, as you can tell. I'm gonna go wash him off and change, back in a few."

She followed me into my private room, which seemed to be normal for her. Most mornings, I woke up to find her standing over me with coffee and donuts, like she lived there, too, so I'd gotten used to her invading my space.

I grabbed some undies, clean jeans and a t-shirt and headed into the bathroom. This time she surprised me by following me right in there, and I turned around and looked at her.

"You mind?" I asked, and she ignored me while she reached under the sink and got me a clean towel.

"Hush, I took these home with me and washed them for you yesterday. You've been using the same towel for a week, and that's just nasty. Use this one."

I took it, and she turned and walked out, closing the door behind her. Sometimes Sylvi reminds me of when I was married, back before the blast. My ex used to take care of me like that, too.

Of course, my ex also filed for divorce a week after getting a look at the new me. Sylvi doesn't let my scars bother her a bit, and even gives me an occasional kiss on the cheek. I think she does it to let me know that she cares what happens to me, and won't let my ugliness get in the way. It helps me feel like a person, so I don't complain.

I showered and washed my hair, watching the red and gray and other colors running out the drain as the remains of a chute-less skydiver came off of me, then got into the clean clothes and went out front. We didn't have any active cases, so Sylvi smiled when I handed her the check for the booze case. Luckily, I'd put it into an inner pocket just before stepping outside, so it wasn't gory.

"Yay, I get paid again this week," she said with a smile. She knew I had enough in the bank to make sure she got paid for a little while, yet, but she liked letting me know she was proud to be part of what was seeming to be a successful PI practice, and I loved seeing that smile, so I didn't mind her little playfulness.

It occurred to me again that day, as it did almost every day that at least a part of me was in love with Sylvi Bouchard. I never told her, of course, because I'm almost fifteen years older than her twenty-two, and besides, girls don't go crazy for guys who've been blazey. I settled for her letting me take her to lunch or dinner now and then, and just enjoyed being able to look at her almost every day.

We spent the rest of the day getting my quarterly tax reports ready to send in, and I winced as I cut the checks for Uncle Sam and the state. It was all part of doing business, of course, just like the premiums I paid for my insurance and bond, but that didn't mean I had to like it, so I didn't.

"Want lunch?" I asked around noon, and Sylvi nodded. "I'm feeling like going out for something, instead of ordering in, that okay with you?"

"Sure," she said, and we headed out to my car. I'd forgotten to take out the blanket when I'd gotten back, so I rolled it up and tossed it into the trunk again. Sylvi wrinkled her nose and said, "That's not gonna smell good in a day or two."

"I'll dig it out and wash it later this evening," I lied, and we got in and headed over to Mancini's, a place that served Italian Beef sandwiches and the best broasted potatoes you'll ever eat! We ordered and sat down to wait for our meals.

Mancini's was one of those places where busy people go for lunch, so they had TV's mounted all over the walls. I was telling Sylvi some old joke when she suddenly gasped and pointed to one of them. I turned, and what did I see but the back of my head, with Mick Mulcahy's face peeking over my shoulder, right there on the Channel Four News. The sound was low, so I couldn't hear anything but noise—my hearing aids help a bit, but all they do is amplify the noise all around me—so, as usual in such situations, I let Sylvi tell me what the announcer was saying.

"Check it out, the announcer says Mulcahy is 'interrogating a witness' who happened to be on site and saw the death of Roger Chittick. He was a dentist, here for a symposium on desensitizing and dealing with hypersensitivity in patients. No information on how he fell, police say there's no sign of foul play in his room. That's about it, except they managed to get a shot of the body as the coroner's people were covering it up. I can see how you got so bloody."

I shook my head in disgust. I hate the news, especially when they try to play on something tragic to boost their ratings. "If you ask me," I said, "the guy came in for his big meeting and had too much to drink. Party and get wasted while you're away from home, and accidents happen."

Sylvi nodded. "Yeah, probably. It's still sad, though. I guess he had a family back home in Joplin, Missouri. Too bad he won't be coming home to them."

That's one of the things I love about Sylvi; she actually has a heart, and I'm gonna try to make sure she doesn't get too burned out on the world and its nastiness, at least as long as she's with me.

We got our food a few minutes later, and ate and enjoyed it. Sadness for people you don't know doesn't stick around long, thank God, so by the time we had finished, we were both in pretty decent moods. We went back to the office and Sylvi made me get that blanket out and take it to the laundromat a few doors down.

Mrs. Wang, the Chinese lady who ran the laundry — yeah, yeah, I know, it's cliche, but that's her name — took one look at it and said, "Two dollah extra, Ned Fain, for blood! It hard to get out!" I paid her with a smile and said I'd be back for it in a few hours.

The rest of the day was boring. I went into my room to watch reruns of my favorite show, "Supernatural," and Sylvi came along with me. We sat on the couch together, me on one end and her on the other, while Sam and Dean and some skinny geek named Garth did their things through a couple of episodes, and when her quitting time came, Sylvi just stuck around to watch a few more episodes with me.

Some days are just better than others, you know what I mean?

The next day was Saturday, and Sylvi had asked a few days earlier if she could have it off to go visit her family. They lived off about two hundred miles away, so it was an all day trip if she wanted to spend any time with them, and I'd said it was okay. Since she was off on Sunday, she was going to stay over Saturday night, and I wouldn't see her again until Monday morning. With nothing much to do, I laid around until past noon, then went out to find a burger and fries and brought them back to eat with Sam and Dean.

It was a nice, easy day, and Sunday turned out almost exactly the same, except for one bad moment when a car caught fire a block away. I dived behind the couch when its gas tank blew, and didn't come out for half an hour. Explosions do that to me, and if you laugh, I will find you. I'm a private eye, remember? I can find anyone.

Three

I woke up Monday morning to find Sylvi standing there, like usual. She was smiling brightly and holding out a big cup of coffee and a bag that I was sure had some of my favorite donuts in it. I smiled back as I tossed off the covers and sat up on the couch in my boxers. Hey, if she was gonna invade my space, she'd have to deal with me being comfy!

Sylvi didn't bat an eye, but then, she'd seen my boxers before in similar early-morning scenarios. She plopped down on the couch not a foot from me and opened the bag as I took my cup from her hand.

"So I had a great time over the weekend," she said, "and I told Mom all about you and how much I like working here. She's scared to death I'm gonna get shot or something, especially after I told her how you saved me from the Electric Axeman, but I said, 'Mom, stop worrying, Ned would never let anything bad happen to me,' and she calmed down a little. So how was your weekend?"

I smiled, thinking about how her mother must think her little girl was working for a lunatic, or some super PI from the cheap novels. Either way, I didn't figure she was going to ever be my number one fan, no matter how much Sylvi built me up.

"It was okay. Watched a lot of TV." I didn't mention the explosion or my resulting panic attack; some things you don't spill to a girl you like.

I got up and went to the bathroom, and slid into some jeans and a shirt while I was there, then we took the coffee and donuts out front. I always liked eating breakfast with her that way, with her sitting across my desk from me. She smiled a lot in the mornings, and that got my day off to a good start even better than the coffee and donuts could do.

We were just finished when the front door opened, and in walked a woman. Did I say a woman? This woman was maybe a bit older than Sylvi, but that was where any similarities ended.

She was about five-eight, had long black hair that hit the middle of her back and a definite Latin look to her features, but it was the incredible figure she sported that I couldn't help noticing. Wow, with a capital WOW! She was wearing a sleek blue dress, and I noticed a necklace that seemed to have a small green stone in it; not an emerald, more like jade.

Now, normally when a potential client comes through the door, Sylvi is instantly up to greet them and get an idea of what they're looking for. This has worked out well for me, because, to be perfectly honest, she does a better job of quoting rates and getting retainer money out of them than I do.

This time, though, I glanced over at her to see if she was going to get up and help this lady, and found her staring at me. Maybe staring isn't the right word—*glaring* might actually fit better, there. I indicated the woman with my eyes, and Sylvi slowly turned and got up.

"Hello," she said, and I thought she said sort of coldly. "What can we do for you?"

The woman looked Sylvi up and down; for a split second I thought I was about to see a genuine cat fight, but then she smiled.

"Hello. My name is Carlota Abreu, and I am an independent reporter for several local news agencies. I've been working on a story about local gambling clubs, and how they get around the laws, and I've run across something that seems to be — well, *sinister* is the only word I can use to describe how it makes me feel. I think I need the help of a professional."

Sylvi didn't even quote her my usual rate of a buck-fifty an hour. She just turned and pointed at the chair she'd just vacated, said, "Mr. Fain can help you," then sat down at her desk with her back to me.

I stood up as she came closer and shook her hand. She got her first good look at my face, and I could see her initial reaction of shock and horror, but she covered it well and sat down.

"Ms. Abreu," I said, smiling. "I'm Ned Fain. Tell me how I can be of service."

She smiled back at me, and it didn't look entirely forced. "Mr. Fain..."

"Ned, please," I interrupted, and she smiled even wider. Over her shoulder, I saw Sylvi stiffen, but didn't know what bee had gotten under her bonnet, so I ignored it.

"Ned," she began again, inclining her head politely, "as I said, I'm doing a piece on local gambling clubs. They

19

get around the state laws against gambling by selling memberships for high fees, and then letting members buy in to different games. They give the members a certain number of chips to play with, depending on the game and the size of the buy-in. When they want to cash out, the club buys the chips back, so there is a semblance of it being only a private club and just for entertainment. However, there is something more going on in one of them, and people are ending up dead. I don't know how to investigate this, so I thought if I could enlist your aid, I might get an even bigger story than I had planned."

I was still smiling. "Well, you've come to the right place, and the right guy!"

She reached across the desk and touched my hand, and I'll confess that it sent a thrill right through me.

"Ned," she said again, and her Latin accent made it sound like something a lot better than my name. "You must allow me to finish. I need to say that I do not have money at this time to pay you, but when the story is done, if I am correct about the suspicious deaths, I'll be able to sell it for a large sum. I can pay you then, even more than you might normally charge."

She was letting one finger rub the back of my hand as she spoke, and I found myself nodding in time with the rubbing.

"That's not a problem," I said, and that was when I saw Sylvi on her feet, standing right behind Carlota. The look on her face was one I'd never seen before, and I couldn't tell if it was shock or fury, but before I could ask what was wrong, she spun around and sat down again. I stared for a second, but Carlota began talking once more.

"I was going to go with a premise about law enforcement having problems with controlling the rise of crime around these small gambling houses. These places that operate as private clubs. They make their money legally, on the surface, through membership fees and buy-ins for tournaments. Since they're considered social clubs, it's legal for the members to gamble there, and some of them are very strict about enforcing the rules. Others are a front for criminal elements, but all of them see a lot of money change hands."

"Okay," I said, "I know a bit about these clubs. Where's the problem with people getting killed?"

"It's at one of the local clubs, one called The Granny Mae Players' Club. I've been going there for a while now, and that's how I stumbled across the killings. First, there was Reuben Zatovich; he was killed by a swarm of bees while he was sitting inside a screened-in patio. He was allergic, and died of anaphylactic shock. Then there was Delila Jewell; she got killed when a radio-controlled airplane supposedly went out of control and hit her in the head. Then the last one was Roger Chittick. He fell..."

"He fell," I said, "from a tenth story window at the hotel he was staying in. I know, he almost landed on me."

Carlota's eyes went wide. "Seriously? That was you? I heard someone was right there, but I didn't know who it was. Anyway, he played at Granny Mae the night before he died, just like the other two. It's like playing there has a curse on it or something!"

So Roger Chittick was one of three people to die after playing at that particular club. Maybe there was more to his death, after all. Seemed a pretty big coincidence, anyway.

I smiled at Carlota. "I think I see why you want help, and I'm in. If this is anything close to involving murders, you'll get a heck of a story, for sure. I'll work with you on it, and we can settle up later on the bill."

Carlota smiled, and I liked that smile. It wasn't like Sylvi's smile, it was more — intense. I liked it, though.

"Ned," she said, "you're a godsend! Between us, I know we can make this work, and get the real story!"

"Okay," I said. "Let me think about how best to tackle this, and get back to me tomorrow. I should have some idea of how to proceed by then."

We shook on it, and Carlota left.

Four

As soon as she was out the door, Sylvi turned around to face me.

"Have you lost your mind?" she asked, and I stared at her with my mouth hanging open in surprise.

"What?" I asked her. "What is your problem?"

"That woman is my problem, Ned! She comes waltzing in here like she's fishing for men, and you gobbled up her bait and agreed to work for nothing!"

I stared at her; I'd never seen Sylvi like this, and I didn't have a clue how to handle it.

"No, I didn't, I just agreed to wait for my fee til she sells her story..."

"And what if there *is* no story, Ned? What if she just fed you a line of crap to get you to do her dirty work, and then she takes the info you dig up and runs with it on her own? You can't prove she made a deal with you! She could cut you out with nothing!"

"Of course I can prove it, you were sitting right there the whole time!"

"Do you think a jury would believe me over her? I can guarantee you that she'd get a lawyer who'd pack the jury with men, and they'd take her word over mine, anytime! I can't save your butt, this time, Buddy!" I sat there and stared at her like she'd grown a new head, but I kept my yap shut. Something told me that Sylvi was really

23

ticked about something else, and I didn't know what it might be, so I stayed quiet for several minutes. Sure enough, after about five minutes of just staring back at me, she let out a sigh and seemed to calm down.

"Okay, so now that you've got yourself into this, how are you going to handle it?"

I hesitated for a moment, trying to figure out exactly how she meant that question. When she didn't say any more, I took what I figured was the most direct approach.

"Well, the first step is to check out this Granny Mae outfit. I need to find out how they operate, and try to get a line on who the big wigs are, the owners or managers."

She nodded as if that was obvious. "So go play poker," she said sarcastically.

I shrugged my shoulders. "One of the things I learned in the Army is that my talents don't extend to gambling. A lot of us lawyers would get together for poker and such, and it was always a foregone conclusion that old Ned was gonna go back to quarters half a payday lighter than when he sat in. A card sharp, I ain't. I'm gonna need to find someone who can actually play at their level."

Sylvi looked at me for a minute, then reached into her desk drawer and came out with a deck of cards. She moved to the chair across my desk and began shuffling them, and I stared at her hands as she did so, because she was making those cards do things I'd never seen before. She shot them all from one hand to another in a stream, fanned the whole deck out with one hand, split them and mixed them over and over with one hand, with two hands, and if I didn't know better, I'd have thought I saw a third hand now and then!

Suddenly, she started dealing cards out, a hand for each of us. When she'd dealt out ten cards, she said, "Let's play some poker."

I picked up my cards and almost fell out of my chair. I was holding four aces and a king. I grinned and laid them out on the desk, but Sylvi gave me a shark's tooth grin of her own and laid her cards down. King, queen, jack, ten and nine of diamonds. A straight flush — my four aces were beaten.

"I paid half my way through college playing cards," Sylvi said nonchalantly. "I can bluff with the best of 'em, and I've always been able to tell when someone else is bluffing; I get a feeling, and it's never failed me yet. You take me to the Granny Mae club, and I'll keep you winning."

I was nodding my head before she finished talking. "Yeah, that's it! Let's do this: you call and find out how we get in, and see if you can get any idea who Granny Mae might be. Could be a name for the company that..."

"Ned, Granny Mae is a nickname for a hand in Texas Hold'em poker. Granny is the queen, and May is the fifth month, so queen plus five equals Granny Mae."

I stared at her for a moment. "How do you keep all this stuff in that little bitty head of yours?" I asked her, and she grinned.

"What, you thought I was a girl? There's a computer in this noggin, buddy boy!"

25

I could almost believe it. Sylvi could come up with trivia that I'd never even heard of on so many subjects that I was thinking of entering her on Jeopardy.

Sylvi called the Granny Mae club and found out that membership cost two grand, but they had an initiation special; a hundred and twenty five bucks for the first week, to see if you like it and want to join. I decided to go for the special, and she told them I'd be in that evening under the name Harry Martin.

We spent the rest of the day working out our plan for the evening. Sylvi taught me the basics of Texas Hold'em, then dug into the bag of tricks she'd had me buy a while back (after I'd gotten a big reward for catching a drug dealer the feds had been after for years) and came up with a gizmo that looked like one of my hearing aids, but was actually a low range radio receiver. With another gadget, the transmitter, tucked into a lacy collar she wore, I could hear the slightest whisper from her in my left ear, which happened to be the one that was damaged the least in the explosion; that one could make out more tones than the right, so I could understand her whispers.

Then we practiced. When you've got hearing loss like mine, it's hard to make out some sounds, so we developed a code for her to use. If anyone overheard her end of it, it would sound like she was humming softly to herself in boredom, but I knew that a soft "dee-dee-*dee*" meant to fold, while "hmm-hmm-hmm" meant raise my bet. We had more than thirty little tunes she could hum, and I'd know what each one meant I should do. I made a mental note to give this girl a raise.

Scratch that note; she already costs me too much money, but I can't afford to be without her. Besides, I'd miss the way she wakes me up.

I sent Sylvi to a costume shop to get us some flashy clothes for the evening, and called Carlota while she was gone.

"Hello?" she answered.

"Carlota, it's Ned. I'm going to the Granny Mae tonight to see what I can find out. Can you give me any names I need to watch out for?"

"Hmm. Arthur Strait, he's the manager, but he never seems to know much of anything. Some of the bartenders like to talk, but once they found out I was a reporter, they stopped talking to me. Just be careful, okay? That place is some kind of dangerous."

I grinned. "I'll be fine. If they won't talk with you around, be sure to stay away tonight. I'll talk to you tomorrow and fill you in on anything I find out." I hung up.

Doggone it, even her voice on the phone was sexy!

Sylvi came back about an hour later, and we took turns changing in my bathroom, since it was bigger than the tiny one in the front office. I was wearing a *very* nice suit, much nicer than anything I could afford to own, and Sylvi looked absolutely stunning in a floor length evening gown. It was blue, with white lace in strategic locations, and if I didn't know any better, I'd have sworn it was designed for her personally. That dress showed off her body better than if it were naked, because every inch of the fabric was stretching and molding around some part of her that I found delightful! She came out of the bathroom and modeled it for me, spinning around so I could see everything.

"Well?" she asked. "Think this is okay?"

I fought down the urge tell her how gorgeous it really was, and said, "Yeah, it'll do fine," but I think she noticed that I couldn't tear my eyes away for more than a few seconds at a time.

We went out for dinner, and since we were so dressed up, I decided to take her someplace nice. I drove us to a restaurant out on the ritzy side of the city, a place called Maurie's, where the clothes we were wearing wouldn't seem out of place, and that's when I got my first shock of the evening.

As I got out of the car and walked around to open Sylvi's door for her—some old habits die hard, and I didn't care how liberated women were; if a girl is with me, I'm gonna open her doors—I could see her checking her lipstick and makeup in the vanity mirror. When she stepped out, she got close and tucked her arm into mine, then leaned up to kiss my cheek. I looked at her, and she whispered, "People at the club have to think I'm your girlfriend, and what if one of the people here is at the club, later? We need to act like lovers, lover-boy, so don't be afraid to cuddle me. I know it's only an act, no worries!"

Okay, I thought, let me get this straight—I actually get to act the way I *want* to act with her, without having to worry about Sylvi being offended, or having it mess up our friendship and working relationship?

Could an evening get *any* better?

Five

We arrived at the club at seven on the dot, and I forked over the buck and a quarter for the initiation. A hostess led us into the place, and I was impressed; it was in an old mansion, and the place was like something out of an early thirties MGM movie, with polished woodwork and marble everywhere.

There were several rooms, and since all of the people who had died had been Hold'em players, we went to the poker room. There, it cost me another hundred to buy into a game (the minimum), and the thought crossed my mind that if Carlota had been coming here as a player, she must have some money stashed somewhere, but I didn't let myself dwell on that. I needed to keep my mind on the game and on Sylvi's codes, so I told myself to focus.

As we sat down, I saw a number of men looking at Sylvi and felt a flush of jealousy, but I reminded myself that she was only my girlfriend for the night. Still, I couldn't resist taking advantage of her willingness to play along, and so I turned to her as the dealer began passing me cards.

"A kiss for luck, Babe?"

Sylvi smiled so big that I almost fainted, and leaned over to press her lips to mine. I was in heaven, but then I passed heaven for the stars as I felt her tongue teasing me, and the kiss turned into one that I knew I'd never forget. As she pulled back a long moment later, she smiled again and said, "Loads of luck, Sweetheart!"

Those men were almost as blown away as I was! If I could read minds, I would only have been more certain of what they were thinking: *How does an incredibly ugly sucker like that get the most beautiful girl in the place?* I had to shake my head to clear it, and turned back to the table.

In Texas Hold'em, you play with two cards that are dealt to you face down, and use them with any of the community cards, that are dealt face up in the middle of the table, to make the best hand of five cards that you can. Sylvi had coached me for several hours, and I had a fair understanding of the rules.

There were six players at our table, five besides me. Four were men, but there was one old woman who looked like she must be in her eighties, and she was grinning at me and Sylvi like she knew a secret. I grinned back, and thumbed up my two pocket cards. I held a Queen and a Ten, and made sure Sylvi, who was leaning her head on my shoulder, got a glimpse of them.

I was to the right of the dealer, being the newest player, so I watched the first round of betting closely. When it came my turn, Sylvi hummed the code to bet, so I tossed in chips to keep me equal to the Big Blind, the minimum bet of twenty dollars. The dealer followed me, and the player to his left checked, so the dealer dealt the flop cards: a Ten, a Four and a Nine. That gave me a pair of Tens for my hand, and Sylvi hummed for me to raise when my turn came around.

Two of the men folded, and when the bet got to me, I raised it to forty dollars. The dealer called, as did the other two players, and I checked.

Next came the turn card, another Ten. I had three of a kind, with a Queen kicker. The other two players bet the minimum, and when it got to me, Sylvi's hum said to raise, so I tossed in four chips, another forty dollars. The dealer called, the old woman called, and the other man folded. It was me, the dealer and the old woman left in the game as the river card was dealt: a Queen. I now had a full house, Tens full of Queens.

The dealer folded, and the old woman laid down one of her cards for the showdown; she had a Four, which gave her two pair. I laid out both of mine, showing my full house, and the pot was mine. Sylvi squealed, grabbed me and spun me around for another kiss I'll never forget, and everyone laughed as the dealer button was passed to the left.

I was up four hundred dollars and change, and nodded to deal me in again. The next game went to one of the other men, and Sylvi had me fold on the flops, because I had nothing to build on. The chance of getting a winning hand without at least one good pocket card and a decent board was very low, so I got out and watched, as she directed. I lost my first bet of twenty dollars, and went into the third game.

This one gave me a couple of good pockets, and the flop was good for me as well. I had two pair, which wasn't bad, as long as no one else could beat it. The turn card took me to another full house, and the river actually gave me four of a kind with an Ace kicker. I took the pot, which had grown to over five hundred, since no one had folded. I was up more than nine hundred dollars, and decided to go once more.

I won again, with a simple two pair. No one else had any luck at all in that hand, and I was now thirteen hundred dollars richer than when I'd come in. I decided to cash out and mingle for a bit, and Sylvi smiled as we wandered toward the bar.

Not being a drinker anymore, I asked for a coke and got it, then Sylvi and I began roaming through the place to talk to folks. I found Arthur Strait, and he was friendly enough until I asked about the owners of the club, then he gave me a blank stare and walked away. I shrugged and looked around for someone else to talk to, and spotted Sylvi flirting with a man who looked to be in his seventies, at least, and fairly drunk. Another flash of jealousy hit me, but then she caught my eye and blew me a kiss, and I mellowed.

I caught a motion from the corner of my eye and turned toward it, just in time to spot Carlota coming in on the arm of some man. I flared, because I could tell that everyone there was looking at her and glaring. With a reporter in the place, no one was likely to do any talking—which was why I'd told her explicitly to stay away—and if she even hinted that she knew me, my own cover would be blown. I looked for Sylvi and found her right beside me, and the look of pure rage in her eyes told me she'd seen Carlota, as well.

I slipped my arm around her and pulled her close like I was going to kiss her, then whispered in her ear, "We might as well go; she's gonna blow our covers if we don't get out of here."

"Yeah," she said, "but gimme a sec!"

She kissed me lightly and pulled away, headed toward the bar. I got a bit ticked that she'd want to get a drink just then, but then I heard her voice in my left ear.

"Hi, there, can you give me an Old Fashioned, with lots of muddled cherries? Yeah, load it up, I love it that way!"

I thought she must be getting a drink for that old guy she'd been talking to, like maybe he'd been helpful and she wanted to give him a reward, but when she got the drink it wasn't his direction she walked in. Instead, she went straight toward Carlota, looking around as if she didn't even know the woman was there, and when she got close, she suddenly turned and ran right into her. The drink, and all that mashed cherry slush, went all down the front of Carlota's white evening gown, and I almost choked on the laughter I was holding back.

"Oh," Sylvi said, "oh, I'm so very sorry! I didn't see you there, please forgive me!"

She turned away without waiting for a reply, and grabbed my arm on her way to the door.

"What," I whispered, "was that all about?"

"Teaching a bee-otch not to mess with your investigations! She knew very well she'd mess things up by coming in, and did it anyway! I wish I'd had tar and feathers, but I had to settle for cherry mash!"

We got outside and into my car without another word. I was sort of mad at Sylvi for what she'd done, but I was absolutely furious with Carlota, so I didn't give Sylvi any grief.

Besides—for one evening, I had been living in the world of my dreams. Truth be told, my biggest fuss with Carlota was that she'd cut it short!

Six

Well, I was up more than a thousand dollars, and I'd had a night I'd never forget, but all in all, it hadn't been a very enlightening evening. I griped to Sylvi a bit about it as we changed back to our own clothes and put the rentals into their protective bags to be returned the next day.

She smiled at me, her best Cheshire-Cat smile. "Don't be such a pessimist, Ned. Remember my old boyfriend, there? His name is Sholto McEwan, and he's quite a talker."

I sat up and looked at her. "Go on," I said.

"Sholto knew all three of the folks who died after playing there. He said they all joined up within a few weeks of each other, and all played Texas Hold'em at the same table we were at tonight. Too bad that's all I got before the bitch showed up."

I sighed. It was something, but not much. "Oh, well. Maybe we can find an association between the victims outside the club. If they all joined around the same time..."

"True. Or I can call Sholto and have dinner with him." She waved a business card in front of my face, and I saw that it had the old man's name on it. "He slipped me this as I was walking away, and asked me to call him and make a date." She was smiling from ear to ear.

I fought down the jealousy, and began to wonder if letting her play my girlfriend had been a good idea, after all. Sure, I'd enjoyed it, but it seemed I was now more smitten than ever, and jealousy would probably only make things worse than they were already. Somehow I couldn't see her finding it endearing if I told the old fart to back off.

"Let's call it a night, and think about this in the morning. I'm not sure calling him would be a good idea; for all we know, he could be working with the killers, might even be one himself. I'm not sure I like the idea of you meeting up with him." I smiled. "Remember, you promised your mother I'd keep you safe, right? Just doing my job, here."

Sylvi looked at me oddly, and I started to feel a little uncomfortable. Was she starting to realize how I felt? If she did, would she stay with me, or quit? I didn't know, and didn't want to think about it.

"Okay. I'll see you tomorrow, then—I guess." She took the clothes with her so she could return them on the way in in the morning, and I went to my room to watch TV. Sam and Dean had all sorts of emotional issues, and maybe I could get some insight from them on how to handle this mess I'd created.

I'd just settled on the couch when my phone rang.

"Hello?" I said, and then I yanked the phone away from my ear.

"I want you to tell that little *cadela* she's got to watch herself, because the next time she decides to mess with me, I'm gonna rip her little *nadegas* into little pieces and shove them all down her throat! How *dare* she dump that *poca* onto me! You tell her I'm going to whip her little *nadegas* until it bleeds!"

That went on for about ten minutes, and I never got a word in edgewise! Finally Carlota hung up, and I said a silent prayer that she wouldn't come in until she'd calmed down.

What on earth had I gotten myself into? As far as I could tell, Carlota was flirting with me to get my help, but I was starting to wonder if Sylvi was some kind of jealous, herself. Between the two of them acting like they were on full time PMS, I was starting to think about a vacation, preferably in some other hemisphere, until they both got over it!

Sylvi didn't wake me the next morning, so I stumbled off the couch around nine. I peeked out front, and there she sat, but her back was turned to me and she didn't look around at the squeak of the door. I closed it again, and went to shower and got dressed.

When I came out, she was still there, and I saw the file Carlota had left with me in front of her.

"Finding anything useful?" I asked, and she turned to look at me then. No smile.

"Not much," she said. "For a reporter, this gal's not too good at digging up much info. I think some of this stuff is made up, to be honest. I mean, she claims that one of the players, someone she supposedly promised not to name, told her that there's a special game where they can bet their lives—I'm having trouble believing anyone would say that to someone they weren't certain of, and especially not to a reporter!"

"That does sound a little farfetched," I admitted, "but it could also be some BS that someone fed her on purpose, trying to discredit her. Why don't you see what you can find out about the three victims, and whether they have any connections outside the club."

She nodded. "I'm on it!"

I sighed. "And, I was thinking—maybe you could call that old geezer and set up a meeting, but somewhere I can be around to watch. I can't take any chances on something happening to you."

Sylvi grinned at me then. "Sure, Boss," she said, and somehow it hurt that she didn't use my name, like she usually did.

The door opened, and in walked Carlota. The two women glared at one another, and I cringed, but neither of them said a word. Carlota stalked over and sat in front of my desk, so I sat down behind it. I looked at Sylvi over Carlota's shoulder, and saw that she was stiff as a board.

"I'm sorry I yelled at you last night," Carlota said. "I shouldn't have done that." I shrugged, but didn't say anything; Sylvi turned her head halfway toward us, then spun it back around to face forward. What was that about?

"Anyway," Carlota went on, "did you find out anything last night?"

"Not much," I admitted. "I was trying to get to know some of the other players when you walked in, and everyone clammed up. I thought I told you to stay away for a while?"

"It wasn't my idea to come there last night, it was my date's. I didn't even know he was a member until he told me we were going there so he could show me off to his friends."

40

Sylvi tossed her head as if laughing at something, and I stifled a snicker of my own.

"You could have begged off, claimed a headache or something. Your being there could easily have blown my cover, and that would make it hard to gain any real information."

"I didn't think about that. Besides, I've been trying to get in with this guy for weeks; he's part of another story I'm working on."

Sylvi suddenly turned and said, "Oh, you're working on a story about prostitution clientele? I bet the research on that is really fun!" She turned back to her computer.

Carlota closed her eyes and I'm pretty sure she counted to ten, before she looked at me and said, "So, I was thinking, why don't we go and look at the crime scenes, where the victims died? We might learn something."

If Sylvi hadn't suddenly clenched her fists, I might have declined, but the sight of her in that mood made me want to get out of the office right away. I said, "Sure, let's go," and was up and on the way to the door before Carlota even realized I was moving. "Your car or mine?" I asked, and when I turned to look back for her response, I also saw Sylvi's face.

It was almost purple, and I didn't wait for Carlota's answer. I got out the door as fast as I could move, but my last glimpse of Sylvi told me that being gone for a while was smart, even if it ticked her off.

Seven

Carlota came out and got into my car, and we drove away. Our first stop would be the home of Reuben Zatovich, because he lived right in the city. She had the address, and I punched it into my GPS. The place was pretty swank, in one of the ritzier neighborhoods in the city, and I was sort of surprised to see a "For Sale" sign beside the driveway.

Carlota read from her notes. "Zatovich died just two months ago, the first one to die the day after playing at Granny Mae. He had a wife and young son, and died of anaphylactic shock after being stung more than a hundred times by honeybees. The bees attacked him inside his screened-in porch." She looked up at the house. "Perhaps the widow could not bear to stay here, after his death."

I nodded toward the driveway. "There's a car; let's go see who's here."

We got out and walked toward the front door, and I rang the bell. A woman of around thirty-five answered, and it was obvious she'd been cleaning.

"Can I help you?" she asked, and the lifeless tone in her voice told me this was definitely the widow.

"Yes, Ma'am," I said. "My wife and I were driving around and saw the For Sale sign, and wondered if we might take a look at the house. We're in the market, and she likes the look of the place."

Carlota smiled at her, and she opened the screen door wide. "Sure, come on in. I was just here doing some cleaning, picking up a few things the movers didn't get. Look around all you like." She turned to go into a room to one side, but I wasn't ready to let her go just yet.

"Oh, so this was your home? Can I ask why you're selling?"

The woman paused, looking down at the floor for a moment before turning back to us. I felt like a heel for making her talk about it, but I needed to know if there was anything she could tell us that would help.

"My husband died here, a couple of months ago. He liked to go and work out on the back deck, that's where he kept his weights and such, and he'd had it screened to keep out bugs because he was highly allergic to bee stings." She took a breath. "That morning, our son was at school, and I went into town for my usual hair appointment. No one else was here, so he liked to work out during that time. Apparently, a swarm of bees got loose from somewhere and got in through a tear in the screen below the deck. The coroner said it looked like the bees came up through the floor boards. By the time I got home and found him, he was dead."

"I am so sorry," I said sympathetically. "You say he was allergic; did he have an epi-pen, or atropine injectors to keep with him?"

She nodded slowly. "Yes. The coroner said he most likely never got a chance to use it, and even if he had, it would probably have been too late. He'd been stung all over his entire body."

"Are there always bees around the area?" Carlota asked, but Mrs. Z shook her head.

"Sometimes you see them around flower gardens, but we'd never seen a hive, or a swarm before. Someone told me a beekeeper in the next county said they might have been from one of his colonies that was splitting, but no one knows for sure."

I thanked her, and we took a walk through the house for appearances, then moved to the deck. I saw the floor boards; there was plenty of gap for bees to come through if they were down there, and a guy doing jumping jacks or bouncing weights around might be enough to disturb them and get them mad. I went out through a back screen door and found where the screen had been torn under the decking. Someone had sewed it up with some fine wire, to close the gap. It was done well enough that I couldn't really tell if the split had been cut, or just gotten torn.

We went back to the car, neither of us feeling much like talking. Carlota gave me the address of the tennis club where Delila Jewell had been killed by a remote control airplane.

"According to the police report," she said as I drove, "Ms. Jewell was playing tennis and a group of radio control airplane fans was using the field across the road for a small air show. One of the people lost control of his plane, and it hit her in the back of her head. The report said she seemed to have died instantly, because the impact was so hard that it took off a lot of the top of her skull."

I drove over to the club and we pretended to be thinking of joining, so a young woman was assigned to give us a tour. Once she got over the shock of seeing my face, she was pretty cool, and seemed more than willing to tell us anything we wanted to know. We saw the courts, the lounges and the grounds, and I mentioned the accident.

"I heard about a lady getting killed here a month or so back. What really happened?"

The girl smiled sadly. "Oh, that was Miss Delila, she was such a sweetheart! She was here almost every week, and was one of the nicest members we had. Some of them can be a little snooty, you know, but she was never like that. Anyway, what happened was one of the RC planes they fly on the open ground across the street got out of control and hit her. I was actually here when it happened, and it was just awful."

I looked across the street. "I'm just not sure I'm comfortable with Babykins, here, playing tennis around something like those airplane freaks. If that happened again, and she got hurt, I'd be just devastated!"

The girl touched my hand in reassurance. "Sir, you don't need to worry. After the accident, our Management Committee bought that field, and it's no longer used for anything like that. I've heard they're going to build a kids' rec center over there, and name it after Miss Delila, and I think that would be wonderful."

"Excuse me," said a voice, and I turned to find another lady standing behind us. "I know the management says it was just an accident, but I was here playing right beside Delila when it happened, and if you ask me, that plane was aimed right at her head! I saw it, and there's just no way you'll ever convince me it wasn't being guided straight at her," she looked at our guide disdainfully, "no matter what *some* people tell you!" Her nose went into the air, then, and she stomped away.

We thanked the girl for the tour and said we'd have to think about it, then left to go to the hotel where I'd seen Roger Chittick fall to his death. Since I'd just handled a case for him, the manager there didn't need a song and dance to let me look around, and took us up to Chittick's room himself.

"Mr. Winston," I asked, "was there anyone with Mr. Chittick when he checked in?"

"No, Sir, he was staying here alone."

I went to the window and moved the curtains to get a good look at it. The bottom edge was about at the level of my waist, so it would be hard to say he fell accidentally. "Any word on how he fell?"

"The police seem to think he committed suicide; that he jumped out the window. It was wide open afterward," Winston said.

Carlota chimed in. "Was there anyone else in the room before he fell?"

Winston hesitated for a second, then said, "There are no cameras in the rooms, of course, but security video captured an unidentified woman getting off the elevator on this floor not long before he seems to have jumped.

47

Unfortunately, there are also no cameras in the hallways, so we don't know where she actually went."

I was about to ask if I could see that footage, when Carlota blew it again.

"Oh, can we see that video? I'm a reporter, we're doing a story on this man's death," she said excitedly.

Winston looked at her for a moment, then turned to me.

"I don't think I can help you anymore, Mr. Fain," he said. "The last thing we need is any more negative publicity. I think we'd better end this discussion, and you should take this young lady and go."

I thanked him, and told him I'd make sure there wouldn't be any flack for the hotel, but he still wouldn't talk any further. I grabbed Carlota's arm and walked her out to the car. When we got there, I pushed her back against it and got right in her face.

"You do not *ever* stick your nose in again when I'm asking questions," I said, "and you will absolutely *never* tell anyone you're a reporter when you're with me! Do you understand me?"

"Ow!" she said, "Ned! You're hurting my arm! Yes, I understand, I'm sorry, alright? I'm sorry!"

I let her go and walked around to get into the car, letting her open her own freaking door. When she got in, I roared out of the parking space and back to the office like I was going to a fire.

Eight

Carlota reached across and touched my arm as I drove, so I glanced her way. "Ned, I'm truly sorry," she said to me. "I got overexcited when he said there was an unidentified woman, and it got the best of me. Let me show you I'm sorry? Let me take you to dinner?"

We were parking at my office when she asked, and I noticed that Sylvi's car was gone. It hit me that she was going to meet Sholto McEwan, and suddenly I was worried about her. She was supposed to make sure I was there to watch over her, but she'd gone on without me.

"Not tonight," I said. "Just go home. And if you can't keep your mouth shut and stay out of my way, then I'm not going to keep working with you on this, got that? Now, go on and leave me be for tonight."

She got out sulking, and I went inside the office. There was a note on Sylvi's desk, and I snatched it up.

Ned,

I got hold of Sholto and I'm going to meet him for dinner. I left some information on your desk. Hope you had a good day,

Sylvi

I grabbed my phone and called Sylvi's cell number, but got no answer. I left a message for her to call me as soon as possible, and then went to look at the printed pages she'd left on my desk.

From what she'd been able to find, the Granny Mae was a pretty legitimate operation. It was incorporated in Nevada, but there was no information on the owners, just the name and address of their registered agent service in Las Vegas. That made me wonder if there might be mob connections; everyone knows the mob runs Vegas, so would it be a big stretch for them to branch out to setting up these private gambling clubs?

The next page was on the three victims. From all the info she could find or hack online, all three of them led pretty normal lives. Zatovich had a few unpaid parking tickets, and Delila Jewell had been arrested ten years before for DUI, but other than those things, they were all squeaky clean. Chittick didn't even have a ticket on his record.

In addition, she could find absolutely no connection between them other than the player's club. As far as could be seen, they didn't even know any of the same people; heck, Chittick lived in another whole city, many miles away.

I tried Sylvi's phone again, with the same lack of an answer. I went over the printouts once more, then tried again. Still no answer, but a minute later she called me back.

"Sylvi!" I said frantically. "I thought you were going to let me know where you were meeting this guy, so I could cover your back? Where are you?"

"Keep it down!" she ordered in a harsh whisper. "Chill out, Ned, Sholto is just a lonely old man who wanted some company, I'm fine! He told me when I called him that he just wanted to have dinner with someone nice, and that was all, so I said okay. I didn't know when you'd be back with that freakin' Amazon, so I came on out to meet him. I'm calling from a stall in the ladies' room. Now chill out, will you? I'll see you in the morning!"

She hung up without another word. I stared at my phone for a moment, then went to my room and turned on Supernatural, season five, episode nineteen. Dean and Sam were at some fancy hotel when they realized that the other guests were disappearing. Turned out that Odin and some other old gods had gotten together there to try to talk Lucifer out of the Apocalypse, and they planned to offer up the boys as bargaining chips. I sat there and cheered them on until they made it safely through the mess, then I shut off the TV and set an alarm on my phone.

I got up at six—an hour that God created only for chickens and dairy farmers, if you want my opinion—and drove to the little down town diner where Mick Mulcahy goes every morning for breakfast. By the time I got there, he was already through his first pancake, so I slid in across from him and ordered coffee and a plate of bacon and eggs.

"Why are you ruining my morning?" Mick asked, and I grinned at him.

"I love you, too, honey," I said in reply. "Just thought I'd join you for breakfast. How you been?"

He shoved a bite of pancake into his mouth. "Can't complain, and if I did, nobody'd listen. You?"

"I'm working on something, a situation with the Granny Mae Players' Club. Know the place?"

"Yeah, and it's not a place you want to get messed up with. Been on our radar for a while, now, but we haven't had the manpower to investigate gambling houses, when we've got murder and drugs running out our ears."

I nodded. "Then you're not aware of the suspicious death connection?"

He stopped chewing. "The what connection?"

"Suspicious deaths. Three of their members have died under strange circumstances the day after playing there. Reuben Zatovich, Delila Jewell and Roger Chittick. Those names ring any bells?"

He shrugged. "Never heard of the first two. Chittick was apparently a jumper. He and his wife were getting a divorce, and I guess he just didn't feel like facing the day. No sign of foul play, his blood alcohol level was way too low to make him drunk, no other drugs in his system; he just took a shortcut to street level. Heck, you were there." He shoved in another bite.

"Zatovich was attacked by a swarm of bees in a screened-in deck he'd built specifically because he was allergic to the little buggers. Jewell was killed by an RC airplane that took off part of her head. Both of them, like Chittick, had played Texas Hold'em at Granny Mae's place the night before they died. I can't find any other connection between them, but something feels off about it, y'know? I was hoping you might take a look and see if there's anything you can share with me."

Mick put his fork down and looked at me. "If I do, you're gonna owe me, right? Like bring me in on the next big headline bust you come across?"

I thought about it, then nodded. "Okay, but one more favor: find out anything you can on an old guy named Sholto McEwan. He's about seventy-five or so, and seems to be rich. He hangs out at the club and seems to know everyone there."

Mick sighed. "I'll see what I can find. I'll call you, don't you call me."

"Deal," I said as my breakfast arrived. We ate together and talked about the weather til he finished and left. When I called for my check, the waitress brought it to me and I saw that Mick had told her I was buying his, too.

Irishmen.

I went back to the office, and Sylvi was there, complete with coffee and donuts. I walked in and said, "Before you say anything, let me say this: I'm sorry I've been such an ass, lately. I don't know entirely why you're so mad at me, but I don't like it, and I want to fix it. Please?"

Sylvi smiled. "Actually, I was going to apologize to you. I've been a total bitch since that woman came in, and I shouldn't be taking it out on you like that. I mean, you're a grown man, you can go after any woman you want, and it's none of my business. Forgive me?"

How I wished it was her business! "No problem, Sylvi, but you got it all wrong. I'm not interested in Carlota except as a client. Frankly, I don't even like the br—the woman. She's not as smart as she thinks she is, and knows exactly when to say the wrong thing and mess up a potentially fruitful questioning."

Sylvi giggled. "Okay. Well, anyway, I went to dinner with Sholto, and he's really nothing but a nice, lonely old man. He didn't even really flirt with me, Ned, he's harmless."

I shook my head. "We can't be sure of that, Sylvi. Like anyone else who's a regular there, he's a suspect in what may be multiple murders..."

That was as far as I got.

Nine

"Ned Fain, I'm telling you he's not a killer, or anything else evil! He spent the whole time we were together last night talking about his wife, who died ten years ago, and his kids; he's a sweet old guy, Ned, and I won't put up with you bothering him!"

"Sylvi, will you listen to..."

"No, not if you're gonna keep being a jerk! He's a nice guy, Ned, so back it off!"

I was about to remind her that I was the boss, there, when the door opened and Carlota walked in. Sylvi and I both turned to her, and at the same time, we both said, *"What?"*

She froze where she stood and stared at us for a moment, then said, "Um, look—I just want to say I'm sorry for all the trouble I seem to have been causing you guys. I didn't mean to, I swear."

For the first time since I'd known her, she actually seemed sincere, and Sylvi and I both mellowed out a bit. I offered her the chair at my desk, and Sylvi pulled hers up close, so the three of us could talk together for once.

I started it out. "I was thinking that we need to pool our notes and see what we actually do and don't know about this case. Make sense?" They both nodded, and looked at me to lead off. "Okay, we know that three people died not long after winning some money at Texas Hold'em at the Granny

Mae. Anyone know what happened to the money they won? Or how much it was?"

Neither of them knew, and I didn't, so I moved on.

"The three of them all died in different ways, Zatovich from anaphylactic shock caused by bee stings; could the bees have been deliberately planted there? Who would have known that his wife would be gone at that particular time? No ideas?"

They shook their heads.

"Okay, Jewell got killed by a model airplane..."

Sylvi held up a hand to stop me. "Nope, this was no model. We're talking about a machine that weighs about sixty pounds, with a four foot wingspan and two electric ducted fans that could take it up to three hundred miles an hour in the air. The nose was made of aluminum, and was sharp and pointy. It hit her hard enough to take off the whole top of her head; she was dead before she knew anything had hit her."

My eyes were as wide as Carlota's. "Ouch," I said. "Any chance the plane was deliberately aimed at her?"

"No evidence it was. The operator was questioned by police, and they said he was pretty broken up about it. From what they could determine, he was one of the newest members of the flying club, and some of the others said they'd told him he wasn't ready for one of the big planes, yet."

I thought about it. Could it be that one of the three was merely an accident, but the others were murder?

"Then we have Chittick. The window ledge was too high to trip, he'd have had to either jump or been shoved over. Was he really depressed over his divorce? Was the woman on the elevator his soon-to-be ex? If so, why was she there, and did she kill him?"

Again, the women shook their heads to indicate they knew nothing. I went on.

"Okay, we have nothing connecting them other than the club, right?"

"Well," Sylvi put in, "Sholto told me that they all played together at the same table on a few occasions. That's the only direct connection I could find for them."

"I wonder if maybe they were running a scam; could be they were working together to share the pots. Someone might take offense at that, and decide to get rid of them."

"But why do them one at a time and so far apart?" Sylvi asked. "In a case like that, I'd think they'd want to stop all of them at once. Exposing them would probably do that as well as killing them."

I nodded. "Unless there was a fourth cheater. Exposure would take him or her down, too. It might be smarter to try to make them all look like they died accidental deaths, like this."

Carlota spoke up for the first time. "Maybe they were winning too much, and the club's manager had them killed?"

I shook my head. "I doubt that. The table stakes aren't that high, and it isn't really affecting the club's profits in any case. The only winnings are taken from the chips the members buy, and there's a premium on the buy-in, so the house always gets its cut."

"Someone outside the group, then? Zatovich's or Chittick's wives, or someone involved with Jewell?"

I nodded. "Possible. Then there's our old friend Sholto McEwan. He seems to know a lot about them and the things that go on there. Maybe he's the fourth member of the team?"

Sylvi glared at me. "Ned, I told you..."

"Just throwin' it out there, Sylvi. One thing I know about killers is that the people who know them are almost always shocked when it comes out; just because he's nice to you doesn't mean anything. If he knows you're working for me, he might be using you to throw suspicion off himself, y'know?"

"Well," she said reluctantly, "I guess that's possible, but I won't believe it unless you show me proof!"

"The main thing we're seeing here, I guess, is that there are more questions than answers in this case. Sylvi, let's try to find out more about those bees. Is it possible we're just looking at two freak accidents and a suicide?"

I turned to Carlota. "You try to find out who was flying that model plane that killed Delila Jewell. I'll look into Chittick."

"Wait a minute," Carlota said. "We're supposed to be working together on this, remember? After all, I'm the one who's paying you!"

"You haven't paid anything, yet, lady!" Sylvi spat, and I interrupted to try to defuse this thing before it went off in my face.

"Carlota, you can do this my way, or on your own. I already warned you not to give me any more problems, so if I were you, I'd shut up and do what you're told!"

She fumed, but got up and stalked out the door. Sylvi glared at her until her car drove away, and then gave me a smile. "Way to go, Ned!" she said, and I smiled back.

Sylvi tracked down Chittick's widow in Joplin, Missouri, and I packed an overnight bag. It was a drive of several hours, so I wanted to get started before it got too late. Sylvi walked me to my car and gave me a hug as I was leaving, and that left me smiling for the first hundred miles. I got in that evening around six, and went straight to the widow's house.

When I knocked, a pleasant looking lady answered the door, but there was something about her that suggested sadness. She didn't bat an eye at my scarred face as I introduced myself.

"Ma'am, I'm Ned Fain, a private investigator looking into your husband's death. Could you spare me a few minutes? I know it's not easy, but..."

She smiled sadly. "Sure, come on in. The kids are at their grandparents' place for the night. I was just having a glass of tea, would you like some?"

I followed her inside to the living room. "Yes, Ma'am, thank you, that'd be great."

She indicated that I should take a seat on her couch, and I did. A moment later, she came back to me with a tall glass of iced tea, and I took a sip. It hit the spot, especially after a long drive and too much coffee.

"Ma'am," I said, but she interrupted.

"Maggie, please."

I nodded. "Maggie, the police think your husband committed suicide, and that he was depressed because you and he were getting a divorce. Is that correct?"

"We were in the process of divorcing, that much is true. Roger asked for it and filed about a month ago, but then last week he called me and said he didn't want to go through with it, and asked me to take him back." She looked out a window. "I wish I'd said yes, but I didn't. He'd been having an affair, I'm pretty sure, and I was still angry over that. If I'd been willing to take him back, he'd still be alive." I saw a tear on her cheek when she turned her face back to me.

"Then you think he killed himself over your rejection?"

She shrugged. "That's what it seems like. See, since it was ruled suicide, I can't collect on his life insurance; but the night before he died, he transferred all his money, including his winnings at the poker club, to our joint account, almost two hundred thousand dollars. That's how much his insurance would have been, so I figure he was trying to make sure I would get it, even though his insurance would be canceled by killing himself."

I thought it over. That did sound like a man who had planned out his own death, and wanted to take care of the wife he had wronged. I asked a couple more questions, but everything seemed to point to suicide, so I thanked her and headed off to find a motel for the night. I settled for one by the Interstate, and the long drive took its toll on me. I didn't even turn on the TV in the room.

Ten

I was up at six, and took advantage of the free continental breakfast (coffee and donuts, of course, but I had a waffle, too) before I hit the road.

There was a lot of traffic, and most of it was going pretty fast. In order to keep up, I needed to push the Mustang a bit, and got it up to about eighty before I was able to stay steady in the fast lane with all the other speed demons out there. The car seemed a bit sluggish, and I made a note to get it tuned up when I got back home.

About a half hour later, I noticed a slightly odd smell, and I thought I heard some loud pinging from the engine, but with my ears, I couldn't be sure. The car seemed to be losing power, and I got irritated at that, so I pushed it a little harder.

"Come on, Baby," I said to the car, "get daddy home and you'll get a whole new set of spark plugs, I promise."

Maybe I should have promised it a turbocharger. A moment later, the engine started sputtering, and suddenly I was in the middle of a three lane highway full of eighty mile an hour traffic with a dead engine and coasting to a stop whether I liked it or not! I threw it into neutral so it would coast as long as possible, turned on my flashers, and started looking over my shoulder for the chance to cut across to the shoulder of the road. I saw a break in the right lane and took it, but I was too slow; I heard the loud air horn just before the semi hit my left rear corner. The car skidded sideways, then began to roll up to the left.

I counted three flips before I blacked out.

I was in a field of some sort, and as far as I could see there was nothing but flowers. I was sitting on the ground, and got to my feet to try to figure out where I was, but there was nothing in sight but more of the flowers, all different kinds. I tried to remember how I'd gotten there, and slowly the wreck came back into focus, and I decided I must have died.

Was I in heaven or hell? Heaven would be this beautiful, but I could imagine being in hell and seeing nothing and no one but flowers for miles, so that I'd be alone forever. I closed my eyes to pray, and that's when I heard Sylvi's voice calling my name. I opened them instantly, and there she was, walking toward me, and I smiled as I ran to her. I was almost able to reach out and touch her when everything suddenly went dark, and I felt like I was in some sort of crushing device.

I realized that my eyes were closed again, and forced them open. There was Sylvi, right beside me, eyes closed and standing over me as I lay—I was in a hospital bed? I raised one hand to touch hers where it lay on the rail beside me; she gasped and looked up at my face and then there was that smile I love so much.

"Oh, Ned, thank God!" she said. "I've been worried sick since the police called me, and all this time—I'm so glad to see you awake! How are you feeling? Does it hurt?"

I tried to speak, but my mouth was so dry I couldn't at first, so I nodded. I tried again, and heard my voice croak out, "Yeah—hurts…"

She patted my hand and reached over for the call button that hung on the rail, then pushed it. "Someone will be here in a minute, just relax. Do you remember what happened?"

I nodded again, and noticed that it hurt like mad to do so. "Car wreck," I said.

"Yeah. I'm afraid the Mustang is *totaled*. The cops say there was bleach in your gas tank, a lot of it. That's why the engine quit. You were going uphill, and the truck that hit you couldn't stop or swerve in time because of other traffic."

I let that seep into my mind. "Bleach?"

"Yeah," she said, "bleach! Someone tried to kill you, Ned. They must have known you'd head onto the Interstate, and figured the bleach would stall you out in heavy traffic."

I nodded, even though I knew it would hurt. If someone was trying to get rid of me, then I was close to something even if I didn't know what it was.

A doctor came in then, and Sylvi stepped aside to let him get close to me.

"Well, well," he said, "it's good to finally meet you, Mr. Fain. You had a pretty close call with the grim reaper, there. I wasn't sure you were going to come back for a bit, there, but this girl," he pointed at Sylvi, "told me that you were the type who would survive a lot worse than this. I guess she was right, eh?"

I tried to smile, but it hurt. "How bad?" I asked.

"Well, honestly, you were pretty lucky. You've got some nasty bruises and lacerations from your seat belt, and there's whiplash and some spinal herniation that'll keep a chiropractor in business for a few months. Your nose is broken, and there are some cuts and bruises on your face, from the steering wheel and all the broken glass."

I licked my lips, then said, "Great. More scars."

Sylvi moved up beside the doctor and smiled at me. "Oh, come on, Ned, like you could get any uglier! These scars might even improve your face a bit, you never know!" She burst into tears all of a sudden. "Oh, God, Ned, they said you had such a bad concussion that you might never wake up! I—I just couldn't imagine life without you! I've been here the whole time, I came as soon as they called, and I drove like a maniac. I got two speeding tickets, but when I told the cops why I was speeding, they cut down the actual amount I was over the speed limit so it won't cost me too much, but I didn't care, I just had to get here!"

I smiled up at her the best I could. "How long was I..."

She reached out and ran a hand across my face. "Ned, you've been in a coma for five days."

Five days? To me, the accident—okay, the wreck—had only happened a few minutes before. The only memory I had since the rollover was of being in that field of flowers, and that only lasted a few moments.

I looked at the doctor. "How long will I be in here?" I asked.

"Well, the biggest concern was the coma. Now that you're awake, if you don't slip back in, I think you can go home in a couple of days. You'll be sore as heck for a while, but with this young lady helping you, I think you'll make out okay."

He left a few minutes later, and I told Sylvi to get me something to drink. She left and came back with a can of root beer, which she knew I liked, and opened it for me. I took a big drink, and it helped a lot.

"I need my phone. I think I've got an idea of what's going on, now, but I need some stuff from Mick."

"Okay, but the doc says I can't let you overdo it. You have to take it easy as much as you can." She dug in a drawer beside me, and handed me my cell phone. The screen had a crack in it, and when I tried to turn it on, nothing happened.

"Here," Sylvi said, "use mine." She handed me her iPhone, and I stared blankly at it until she took it back. "Mick Mulcahy, right?" she asked, and I nodded as she dialed his number. I didn't even know she knew it, but then I'm always surprised at what she knows.

"Mick? It's Sylvi. He's awake and wants to talk to you." She handed me the phone and I put it to my left ear.

"Mick, tell me what you got," I said, and he began to fill me in on what he'd learned about the victims and Sholto McEwan. When he was done, I thanked him and promised to meet him for breakfast again soon, then gave Sylvi back her phone.

"Do you have your computer?" I asked her, and she nodded. "Good. I want you to tap into Roger Chittick's bank records, and then get into the Excelsior Hotel's security camera system. I know it's connected to the internet, because

I hooked into it when I was working on the booze case. There's footage somewhere in there that shows a woman getting off the elevator on Chittick's floor the morning he was killed. I want to see that tape."

She smiled. "Yeah, you're back," she said, and then she leaned down and kissed me right on the lips. I was startled, but she only giggled when the machines monitoring me signaled a rise in my heart rate and blood pressure.

Eleven

I got out of the hospital two days later, as the doctor had said, and Sylvi drove me home in her little Scion. It was still a long drive, but between the Tramadol and being with Sylvi, I made it through with no real problems other than walking with a cane. We were able to leave early, so we got to the office around five that afternoon, and Sylvi helped me into my room. I settled in on the couch while she turned on the TV and got it on Netflix for me, then went to get us something to eat for dinner. She came back with a large supreme pizza and a six pack of root beer in bottles. What a girl!

We ate together, and watched a couple episodes of Supernatural; Sylvi admitted she was really getting into the show, even though she'd never seen it on regular TV. When we finally turned it off it was getting near ten o'clock.

"You can go on home," I said. "I'll be fine tonight." She'd been sleeping in a chair for a week, there in my hospital room, and I figured she would want to get home and get a real night's rest.

"Are you nuts? I'm not letting you outa my sight! Move over, this couch is wide enough for both of us!" She pushed me over so I was laying down, and the next thing I knew she was laying there with me, her back to me, and pulling the blanket I used up over us. I didn't know what to do.

"Sylvi," I began, "um, look—this isn't a good idea. I mean, don't get me wrong, you're making me feel good that you care enough to want to stay and take care of me, but— well, us sleeping like this, that's not..."

She rolled her head around so she could look at me. "Why? You afraid you'll get over excited? Well, relax, we're not going there, but I'm staying right where I am, so chill out and get some sleep. Need a pain pill?"

I sighed. There wasn't going to be an easy way out of this.

"No, I don't need a pill," I said, "but you still can't stay. Sylvi, look—I love having you working for me, and I know you know I like seeing you, looking at you every day—but this is only going to mess with feelings I'm keeping shoved down deep."

Her eyes were boring directly into mine. "What feelings, Ned? You mean the feelings you have that make you think about what if we were together? The feelings like what if those kisses I gave you last week at the club were real? Those feelings? Do you think I'm stupid? I know you have a thing for me, Ned, and it's fine."

I shoved her off onto the floor all of a sudden, and she squealed in protest. "No, Sylvi, it is *not* fine! Look at me! Do you think I don't know how damned ugly I am? I'm going through every single day of my life, in love with the most beautiful girl I've ever known, and knowing that no matter how much you like me, or care about me, you could never love me, because I'm a freakin' scarecrow! And I haven't said that before because I know that it'll cause problems for us, and I can't handle that, I can't handle the thought of you not being there in the office, not waking me up in the mornings, not..."

She was up on her knees, leaning close, and she kissed me again. "I know, Ned, I know. But guess what? When I look at you, I don't stop at the scars; I look into your eyes. Remember that first day we met? When you came in here looking to rent the place? I looked into your eyes then, and that's why you weren't able to get rid of me. There was something about you, something special, and I didn't know what it was, but I wanted to find out. And then, when the Electric Axeman had me, and was threatening to kill me? I knew, I *knew*, that you were going to come save me. I knew it!" She kissed me again. "I know you love me, Ned, and I'm just as much in love with you. I'm not here because I'm worried you'll fall and hurt yourself, tonight; I'm here because I need to feel you close to me. I don't know where we're gonna go from here, but I promise I'm not gonna run away. Okay? Now, can I get back on the couch with you? Please?"

I stared at her for a long minute, then lifted the blanket and let her crawl in. She snuggled back to me, and I put my arms around her and just held her until we both drifted off to sleep.

When morning came, we got up and went to the diner to have breakfast with Mick, then grabbed our coffees and donuts and took them back to the office. We had them at my desk, like we usually did, and talked about the same nonsensical things we always talked about for a while, just enjoying being in each other's company.

However, life isn't all about fun and games, so at nine I had Sylvi call Carlota and ask her to come by so we could go over some of what we'd learned. She agreed and said she'd be there in half an hour.

She showed up right on time, and we all gathered around my desk, Sylvi with her computer on her lap.

"Okay, here's what I'm thinking," I said. "At first, we thought all three of these deaths were related because the victims were all connected to the same club. Thing is, I had Sylvi do some additional digging, and we found out that Zatovich's gardener told him two weeks earlier about the rip in the screens under the deck, and it was even on their schedule to fix it when they came back the next time—which would have been the day after he died. They did fix it, by the way, that's why it was sewn up when we saw it."

She nodded. 'Okay, but what about the other two?"

"Ah, Delila Jewell. The police questioned the man who was operating the plane that killed her, and found out that he was a novice at the sport. He should never have been trying to fly a plane that big with no more experience than he had. He lost control and panicked, and even though the police say it was an accident, his failure to abide by certain safety rules led them to charge him with involuntary manslaughter. He's facing up to fifteen years in prison; if he had been hired by someone to kill her, I think he'd be singing his head off, now, and if he was the actual killer himself, then who could have killed Roger Chittick? No, this was just another freak accidental death." I smiled at her.

"Then we come to Roger Chittick. Roger seems to have killed himself because he was despondent over his wife refusing to take him back after he filed for divorce. She thinks he was having an affair, so when he asked to stop the divorce, she refused. Poor guy must have figured his life was already over, so he did himself in."

"Why do you say that?" Carlota asked. "Maybe the wife killed him, if she thought he was cheating."

I nodded. "I thought of that, too," I said, "so I got Sylvi to hack into the hotel's security system and find the footage of the unidentified woman who got off the elevator that morning. You wanna play that for us, Sylvi?"

"Sure, Ned," she said and put the computer on the corner of my desk. She touched a control, and the video began to play. The camera view showed the elevator area, a section of hallway with the two elevators side by side in the fish-eye view. One of the elevators opened, its twin doors sliding apart, and a woman stepped out. She was wearing slacks and a long sleeved shirt, and a light jacket was draped over her shoulders with the sleeves tied together around her neck. She had the jacket's hood over her head, so her face couldn't be seen. She was only in view of the camera for a second, and then was gone.

Carlota was watching it intently, and when it was over, she seemed to sigh in relief. "So who was that?" she asked. "Do we know if it was the wife?"

I shook my head. "No, it wasn't the wife. Sylvi and I watched that strip over and over, and finally we started going over it one frame at a time. Show her what we found, Sylvi."

"With pleasure," Sylvi said with a smile, as she called up another program. This one showed the same scene, but it was bigger and frozen at the point where the woman was beginning to step out. Sylvi tapped something with a finger, and the scene advanced by one frame. She tapped again, and again, until the woman was fully in view of the camera.

I leaned over and pointed at the woman's neck. "See that?" I asked Carlota. "That's a necklace, and the stone hanging from it is identical to the one you're wearing right now."

Carlota looked at me, and I saw a mixture of panic and rage start to build, but she was keeping it in check.

"Here's what I think happened, Carlota. I found out that Chittick has been coming to the Granny Mae for the past few months, anytime he was in town on business. I figure you met him there when you first began working on your story, and the two of you hit it off. You started an affair with him, which probably got even hotter after you saw that he was winning big a lot. I wonder, did he offer to take you away with him somewhere? Leave his wife and kids for you?"

Carlota sat there and said nothing, so Sylvi chimed in. "Yeah, that's probably what happened. But then, somewhere along the line, Roger got tired of you, didn't he? Maybe he saw that it was more his money that turned you on than he did, and he realized he'd gotten into something he wanted out of, so he asked his wife to take him back. He'd obviously had enough of you, I mean, *sheesh*, he didn't even want to spend any money on you! He gave it all to the woman he truly loved, his wife! He probably figured that once she saw that, she'd take him back, that she'd believe he was sincere. You sure weren't worth that much to him; heck, you weren't worth more than a night or two in a hotel bedroom to him! You weren't his woman, you were only his sex toy!"

"*Shut up!*" Carlota screamed at Sylvi. "You don't know *anything*! Roger loved me, he told me so, over and over! He filed for divorce for me!"

"Yeah, he did," I said, "but somewhere along the way, the guy changed his mind, didn't he. He told you he was going home, going to try to save his marriage, right? And you couldn't have that, now, could you?"

Sylvi took over. "So you went to his room, you probably called and told him you were coming to say goodbye, right? He let you in, and you got him over by the window, and when you saw your chance, you pushed him over the edge and watched him fall!"

Carlota caved, and she began sobbing as she talked. "*No*, it wasn't like that. Yes, I went to see him, but I wanted to try to get him back, not hurt him. We talked, but then he said no, he was going back to *her*, and I got mad. We had an argument, and he went over to the window to calm down — and I didn't mean to, but I pushed, and he fell, and it was too late to take it back..."

75

"So you saw Ned, there, when he witnessed it," Sylvi said, "and you figured if you got him involved, he could be your stooge if the cops started to figure it out, right? But when Ned went to see Chittick's widow, you knew he'd start to catch on, and so you decided to follow him and try to get rid of him, too! Right?"

Carlota looked at me, still with tears running down her cheeks. "I'm so sorry. It all just got so out of control, I didn't know what to do..."

Mick Mulcahy stepped out of my private back room and walked up to her. "Carlota Abreu, you are under arrest for the murder of Doctor Roger Chittick, and the attempted murder of Ned Fain. You have the right to remain silent..."

Twelve

The next couple days were a bit rough. Carlota detailed under questioning how she had followed me to Joplin and put the bleach in my tank. She was hoping I'd get killed on the freeway, another death she could point to as being connected to the Granny Mae, since I'd played there, too. It would have been easy, she thought, and would stop me from finding out about Chittick's affair. She knew that would eventually lead back to her, and it did.

Sylvi and I were still not talking about what had happened the night we got back, the night she said she loved me. I was afraid to bring it up, because what if it was a tramadol-induced dream? If I imagined it, I wanted to keep that my secret. The night after we exposed Carlota, she'd gone home at her usual time like nothing out of the ordinary had happened, so I didn't say a word.

She woke me the next morning in the usual fashion, a tall cup of coffee with tons of sugar and a bag with four donuts in it. We ate them at my desk, and then started going through the bills that needed to be paid. If I hadn't won that thirteen hundred, things would have been pretty tight already, but I'd survive another week or two before I had to break into my reserves in the bank.

On the other hand, I was looking at needing a chiropractor soon, and they weren't cheap. I didn't have any health insurance, so I'd have to find a way to pay for it myself, and that would wipe out those reserves fairly quickly. Something needed to give, and soon!

The door opened, and in walked Sholto McEwan. Sylvi and I were both surprised, but she got up and went to hug him.

"Hey, Mr. McEwan," she said. "You okay?"

"Oh, I'm fine, my dear girl," he said, with a thick Scots-like accent. "I merely stopped in because I'd like for your Mr. Fain to do something for me."

Sylvi looked at me and the look said I'd better play nice.

"Mr. McEwan," I said, "it's a pleasure to meet you, finally. What can I do for you, sir, and does it involve driving or getting hurt? I'm not much up to either, at the moment."

The old man smiled at me. "Won't be a problem," he said. "In fact, all I need is for you to take a deposit to the bank, if you will." He held out a paper and Sylvi took it from him to look at it, but then her face went white and she passed it to me. I was a check, made out to me, for fifty thousand dollars!

I looked up at the old guy, and he was smiling. "Mr. McEwan, I don't understand."

"Aye, and it should be simple for a private eye, now," he said. "The Granny Mae Clubs, the whole franchise of 'em in eleven states, belong to me, Laddie. That woman and her stories about people dying in my clubs, that could have been very bad for business, you know. Yer own exposin' of the truth has saved me quite a fortune, and that is just a small part of it, to show you my gratitude!"

I didn't know what to say, but Sylvi came to the rescue. She reached up and pulled the old man's cheek down to her and kissed it sweetly, then turned to me and said, "Didn't I tell you he's just the sweetest guy?"

He blushed, but he looked right at me. "Me, a sweetie? Nah, don't you believe it, Laddie! But there is one more thing; I heard how that woman did in your car, so it occurred to me you might be needing one. I had this in my collection, and felt it might do you well."

He handed me a fob with a set of keys, and then took Sylvi's hand to lead her outside. I naturally followed, and there at the curb was a limousine with his chauffeur standing beside the rear door. I looked at him in confusion.

"Oh, no, not that one," he said with a chuckle, then pointed behind the limo. "It would be *that* one I'm speaking about!"

There at the curb sat a Mustang. I almost fell over as I slowly walked toward it, and ran my hands across its beautiful lines. This wasn't a late model version like the one I'd just lost, you see…

This was a 1969 Mustang Cobra Jet, the original Boss Mustang! I stared for a long moment, with Sylvi standing close to me and smiling from ear to ear, then looked at Sholto.

"Mr. McEwan, I can't accept this," I said, but he waved me off.

"As I said, Mr. Fain—'tis nothing compared to what you've saved me. Enjoy it in good health, but be careful with it. She's a bit like your Miss Sylvi, she is—there's a lot of power in her!"

The end.

If you enjoyed this story, please leave a review. Your words really mean a lot.

Get a FREE *unpublished* Ned Fain story and be among the first to hear about Sam's new book releases and special deals when you join his email list here:

http://www.mix-booksonline.com/sam-abbott-insiders

Get more adventures with tough, sometimes cynical private eye, Ned Fain for one low price:

Ned Fain Private Investigator Series: Books 1 - 6

And see all of Ned's books here:
http://www.mix-booksonline.com/category/sam-abbott

Sam Abbott

…is a pseudonym for a popular author of adventure and cozy mystery. Who is that, you ask? Well, that's another mystery.

Join Sam on his facebook page:
https://www.facebook.com/SamAbbottAuthor

If you enjoyed this book, you might like these from author Liz Dodwell:

- Adventure/Mystery – **The Captain Finn Treasure Mysteries:**
  - o The Mystery of the One-Armed Man
  - o Black Bart is Dead
  - o The Gold Doubloon Mystery
  - o The Game's a Foot
- Adventure/Mystery – **The Agency Confidential series:**
  - o Deceit
  - o Cheat

Made in United States
North Haven, CT
03 October 2024

58205040R00046